U've Been Served

U've Been Served

Brenda G Melton

ISBN: 0996581405
ISBN 13: 9780996581400

Official Notice of Invitation

I,_____(The Host),

being of sound mind and under no duress,

do hereby certify, attest and affirm the following:

_____(The Invitee)

is invited to appear at_____(address/location)

on_____(date) at_____(time)

to celebrate the happy divorce/uncivil disunion/decoupling (circle one)

of_____(The Divorcee).

By order of the court, please RSVP.

I now affix my signature to this notice this___date of___, 20_____.

_____

Host's Signature

U've Been Served!

Dedication

This book is dedicated to all the women that have gone through a divorce or are currently going through the process. May you find peace and healing through laughter!

Acknowledgements

TO MY DEAR FRIEND, TARA, for inspiring me to serve up the humor, bringing hope and support to all women that have endured such difficult times in their lives.

To Alisa, who unknowingly acted as my muse during many late-night conversations.

And last but not least, to my loving husband, Phil, who fortunately never served up anything but support and kindness in our 20 years of marriage.

A special mention for my dear friends, Ginger and Rosemary, who always said, "His thyme was a-cumin!"

Introduction

I DON'T NEED TO TELL you that divorce is unpleasant. Any woman who has been or is currently going through a divorce knows that it is one of life's most personal, painful experiences. The concept behind *U've Been Served* came to me while visiting a dear friend who, after three children and 25 years of marriage, had been served with divorce papers. Suffice it to say, she needed to vent, and it was this venting session that planted the seeds for the book.

During our long talk, I was stunned to witness the transformation of my usually tranquil friend. This was not the quiet, unassuming, self-controlled woman I'd known most of my life! Fuming with expletives and adjectives I never knew she possessed, what came out of her mouth was shocking and so unlike her. Clearly, she had been pushed to her limit! It's amazing what stress, betrayal, and rejection can reduce us to.

To add insult to injury, while she had previously gotten along quite well with her mother-in-law, enjoying accolades like "good mother" and "great cook," battle lines had been drawn, and she now found herself in enemy territory. To her dismay, the praise she'd once enjoyed was now a thing of the past. In order to keep this book PG, I'll refrain from using any of the extremely colorful expletives, but here's a small taste of what it sounded like: "I'd like to take his (*bleeping*) balls, fry them up in a pan, and serve them for dinner when his mother comes to visit next week! I'll show *her* some creative cooking!"

While I eventually recovered from the shock of seeing my friend in that state, my mind couldn't help but repeatedly wander back to the vivid image of fried balls, which led to images of limp noodles and fried balls—better known as spaghetti and meatballs—as well as limp noodles and *no* balls, and other funny culinary offerings. Before I knew it, what had started as a simple attempt to comfort my friend, blossomed into an opportunity to create a hilarious series of silly recipes, toasts, and party ideas designed to help lighten the load of women everywhere who are going through this most difficult time in their lives.

Many of those early recipes and ideas have been incorporated into this book. It's important to note that this is not a cookbook, so if cooking isn't on your top-10-skills list, don't despair. The recipes included here are simple to make using ordinary, everyday ingredients. (In fact, take-out is my specialty!) *U've Been Served* offers an opportunity for friends to gather together and provide a platform for support, recipes for laughter, and toasts to a new beginning.

Many of us look at divorce as a failure to manage our lives or family, calling into question the integrity of our character. As a divorcee myself, that was exactly how I felt. Now I can look back at my divorce as a valuable teacher. For the past 20 years, I have been happily married to a wonderful man and my best friend. Obviously, my failure—or, *lesson learned*—led to a happy ending—or, *happy beginning*!

A year before I started writing this book a very dear friend was going through a divorce. Alisa and I hadn't been in contact due to the abusive nature of her relationship with her now-ex. I hate to admit it, but we were out of touch for two years. One day I ran into her in a department store, and it was as if those two years were yesterday. We hugged and immediately started reconnecting. Within minutes, I knew something was different. She seemed confident and happy. Alisa told me the news I'd been hoping to hear: She had filed for divorce, and it was almost final.

"Let's have lunch and catch up!" I said.

"What are you doing now?" she replied.

At a nearby restaurant, we ate, drank a bottle of wine, laughed, cried, and created new memories. I realized that my friend was going to be OK. Alisa understood our separation and knew that she had to take ownership for her choices in life and in love.

During the weeks and months that followed, Alisa became a late-night muse for the book, and I was her sounding board that helped her navigate the divorce process and accept that her marriage of 20 years was finally over. I'm not a late-night person but I knew my friend needed a non-judgmental ear, so once or twice a week, Alisa would call, usually after 10 p.m., and we would both pour a glass of wine and chat for hours on the phone. Without realizing it at the time, she provided much of the material needed to finish the book.

I recall one particular conversation when Alisa mentioned that she'd like to start dating again. I forget exactly how the conversation went, but somehow she uttered the words, "I'd love to have a few dates lined up." My mind immediately went to *U've Been Served*, and I grabbed a pen and paper.

"What are you doing?" Alisa asked.

"Dates are a food item and could be a party favor for my book," I said.

"What book?"

"A book I'm writing on behalf of women going through the exact same thing you are: divorce!" I said, sharing some of my recipe titles.

"What a great idea! I'll have the first party," she said, laughing hysterically.

Alisa loved it so much that every time we talked on the phone she had more content for the book. I told her that our conversations and the information she was providing was free therapy—the perfect recipe of laughter and friendship!

The most common question about *U've Been Served* is, "Why would you not make this book more gender-friendly? After all, divorce, cheating, and humiliation are not just women's issues." Of course you are correct. If I felt that men would have a party, buy the book, and support their friends as women do, I wouldn't have hesitated. But most men are molded differently. The majority of the time, a man will pick up their friend from the courthouse steps, go to a bar, and say, "We need to get you laid. Time and healing doesn't matter. Get back on that horse and start riding again."

If you or someone you know has a sister, mother, or good friend that needs your support, I urge you to gather the girls and enjoy a *U've Been Served* party. Whether it's breakfast, lunch, or dinner, the main course is healing, and I can think of no better cure than laughter. Remember to end your breakfast, lunch, or dinner party with an inspirational message.

Eat up and have fun. U've Been Served!

How to Plan a *U've Been Served* Party

Hosting the Party

Throwing a *U've Been Served* party couldn't be simpler. With minimal planning and a few good friends, the party is on! There are no complicated recipes here. Many of the food selections are everyday dishes that most people can prepare easily or buy premade. Or, you can host the party at a nearby restaurant. Whether planning the party for yourself or a friend, the main objective is to get the girls together to express love and support.

Your party can be as simple or as elaborate as you want it to be; it's limited only by your time, budget, and imagination. The key ingredients: Keep it light, encouraging, and most of all fun! The main objective to having a successful party is to be very creative with little or no effort.

Review the menus and glossary of food terms to help you decide which foods would best describe what you want for your party, keeping in mind the divorcee's personal experience. For example, if the divorcee's husband was a cheater and you want to have a

U've Been Served breakfast party, you could order or make *Cheater Cheater Egg Beaters* (because one woman was never enough) with bacon (pig) and a side of *you're toast*. For a luncheon, serve *Dog in Heat* (never could keep his paws to himself) and a bag of Lay's potato chips. If dinner is more your style, try *Filet of My Soul* (filet of sole) with a side dish (mistress) of *too-wild* rice and *oh-no-you-didn't-lay-her* cake for dessert.

Taking the party to a restaurant

This is my personal favorite and could add so much fun and creative thinking to the party. Once you know the number of guests, be sure to call your restaurant and reserve a table. Everyone will order from the menu in a creative, *U've Been Served* style. It would be helpful to bring a copy of the book to the restaurant. Party invitations are optional.

When ordering, refer to the *U've Been Served* glossary of terms. For a steak say, "mis-steak," and to order fish say, "caught in the act." You get the idea. *Limp noodles and no balls* is spaghetti with meat sauce. Potatoes are *twice-baked* with *not-so-sweet, whipped* butter. Get a *tossed* salad—make it a Caesar. And for dessert, it's *bittersweet* chocolate cake.

Your party can be as intimate and simple as going to the nearest bakery and buying a *not-so-sweet* pie or *bittersweet* chocolate cupcakes and bringing them over to the divorcee for a laugh. Invite some of her closest friends or just keep it private between the two of you. I guarantee you are bound to make her day.

Think about it, if you were to go over to your friend's with a *U've Been Served* book and a *not-so-stiff* lemon meringue pie, don't you think that it just may be the one thing that would get her ass out of bed? If not, you tried!

I wish I would have had this idea four years ago when it was almost impossible to get my best-friend out of bed for dinner, much less out of the house. You can't change what is, but with a little fun and humor, you can make it easier for your friend or family member to get through what is one of the most difficult times of her life.

Creating your menu

Planning the menu for a *U've Been Served* party can be almost as much fun as hosting the party itself, and it's as easy as a short trip to the grocery store or a local fast food restaurant! Provided are a number of menu selections, together with simple recipes to create *U've Been Served* dishes for breakfast, lunch and dinner. Each of them represent a variety of personality types or situations; but don't limit yourself. Select the dishes most appropriate to the situation, or feel free to adapt them as you desire. Remember, it's *creative* cooking! Once you've made your selections, you can create your own *menu*. Then sit back and watch your guests laugh their asses off as they are *served*!

Preparing the guest list

Determine who you'll be inviting to the party, and then schedule the time, date, and place for your party. You may want to host it in a private home, or if you think the girls would benefit from a night on the town, you could host it in a restaurant.

Once you've put the date on your calendar, you're ready to send out your *U've Been Served* invitations. Make certain to send them out at least two weeks in advance and to include an RSVP. You'll want to know how many people you'll be serving and, if this is a joint effort, who will be bringing what.

Suggested party favors and ideas

A Box of Dates

If you are hosting a *U've Been Served* party, ask all of the guests to bring a box of dates. Not only are they high in fiber and rich in nutrients, but it's good to know that when and if the timing is right and you are ready to date again, your friends and family have their eyes and ears open for that special someone.

Sour Grapes

Buying wine can be an adventure and a party in itself. Go to your nearest specialty wine store, and check out all the colorful names and labels like *Fat Bastard*, *Bitch*, and *Mad Housewife*. One is bound to suit your specific *U've Been Served* party. I like to call it the *Total Whine Experience*, in recognition of Total Wine & More, one of my favorite wine stores where I've spent hours looking, laughing, and buying.

Custom Printed Toilet Paper

Turnabout is fair play. After all, you were dumped on for how many years? Google "personalized or custom-printed toilet paper" to get a few rolls with your ex-husband's picture all over them. They usually take five to seven business days to produce.

Menu Selections for Breakfast, Lunch and Dinner

ALL OF THE MENU SELECTIONS can be modified to your specific party. I give you suggestions, but this book is about being creative and thinking outside the box. Have fun!

Breakfast Menu

For broken egg-spectations.

CHEATER, CHEATER EGG BEATERS

For the ex who thought one woman was never enough.

Served with bacon, *too-fresh* berries, *you're toast* with K-Y jelly, and French grind (*also known as the blonde roast from Starbucks*)

SCRAMBLED EGGS

For the ex who could never make up his mind.

One, two, or three scrambled eggs, served with *miniature* sausages, *too-fresh* berries, *you're toast*, and *ex*-presso or French grind.

GETTING-OVER-EASY EGGS

For the smooth-talker that never thought I'd figure it out.

Two eggs over *really* easy served with lots of *beggin'* and your choice of *too-fresh* berries or mixed fruit, and *ex*-presso or French grind.

Hard Boiled Eggs
For the hardhead you'd love to crack. (The other head was never hard!)

Served with *you're toast, I Can't Believe it's Not Buttered, miniature* sausages, and *ex*-presso.

Egg McNuthin'
For the good-looker without an ounce of substance.

A toasted English muffin topped with cheese, Canadian bacon, and *nuthin'* else! Served with *no-passion* fruit or *too-fresh* berries.

Ex-Benedict
For the traitor who kept switching sides.

One large *ex* on a toasted English muffin topped with cheese, Canadian bacon and Hollandaise sauce.

Sowing His Wild Oats
He sowed 'em; you eat 'em.

Steal-cut oatmeal served with *crazy-ins, mixed-up* nuts, *too-fresh* berries, *you're toast*, and French grind.

YOGURT
Cultured? That was always debatable!

Add mixed berries.

HOT-AND-COLD DRINKS
For the relationship that was always off and on.

FRENCH GRIND
French Maid? Au Pair? Just coffee, girls. Get your minds out of the gutter!

EX-PRESSO
For the one-minute man. (No explanation needed!)

NOT-SO-HOT CHOCOLATE
For the guy who was always lukewarm.

Top with *whipped* cream.

ORANGE-JUICE-GLAD
A little bit of sunshine, freshly-squeezed with lots of pulp.

CRAMMED-BERRIES JUICE
For that tangy yet somehow sweet aftertaste.

MORNING INSPIRATION
We all have *egg-spectations* and dreams of what life should be. Today, I *egg-spect* nothing more than to have gratitude and love

for the family and friends that support me through this difficult time.

Boner-Petite!

Lunch Menu

'Cause I'd like to eat his.

FINGER SANDWICHES

A sign-language salute to the guy who did you wrong.

This dainty assortment of creatively cut finger sandwiches is more than just a meal. It's a moment! Finger sandwiches can be any sandwich—bologna, ham, or cheese, for example—that you cut to your desired size and shape.

FULL-OF-BOLOGNA SANDWICHES

For the ex who never told the truth a day in his life.

Place a slice of bologna on your choice of bread. Add cheese and *condom-ents* at no extra charge!

Po' Boy Sandwich

For the couch potato who never wanted to work . . . Po' Boy.

Two slices of white, cheap bread and nothing inside!

Hamming It Up

For the ex whose ego was bigger than his . . . well . . . you get it.

Ham on whole wheat or white bread with your choice of Swiss, American, or cheddar cheeses.

Grilled Cheesy

For the ex who was never authentic a day in his life.

Served on *you're toast*, grilled and buttered, with your choice of American, Swiss, or cheddar cheeses.

Sloppy Joe

For the ex who thought I'd always be his maid.

Maid-to-order, extra-sloppy Sloppy Joe sandwich, served on a sesame seed bun.

Dog In Heat

For the tail-wagger who never kept his paws to himself.

These *enormous* wieners are served thoroughly *cooked* to order: your choice of boiled, broiled, grilled or fried. For a little extra fun, chop the hot dogs into pieces!

WRAP IT UP
It's a wrap! The divorce is final!

Served with a warm hug and your choice of wrap (spinach, sun-dried, or whole wheat), with turkey, ham, or chicken.

HOT-AND-COLD DRINKS
For the relationship that was always off and on

ASSORTED SOFT DRINKS

LEMON-AID

ICED TEA

AFTERNOON INSPIRATION
Life is what we make it and how we choose to move forward. This afternoon, I choose to nourish my soul and body with love and laughter.

Boner-Petite!

Dinner Menu

Many of these recipes are perfect for an outing with the girls. Although most restaurants will have these food items on their menus, they probably won't be as colorfully described as the *U've Been Served* format, but this would be great conversation for everyone at the table. After a few bottles of *sour grapes* or *I-call-the-shots-now*, you are sure to disclose why you selected the *menu*.

Chicken

SPINELESS, BONELESS CHICKEN BREASTS
For the coward who never stood up to mother. Last I heard he was still nursing!

Make it grilled, fried, or using your own special recipe, just as long as the chicken breasts are boneless and fully cooked. Serve with *twice-baked* potato, *beet-it* salad, and for desert, a *not-so-stiff* lemon meringue pie.

JERK CHICKEN
For the jerk who was never capable of spicing up anything!

Could be breasts, thighs, drumsticks or wings cooked any way you like, so long as you apply the jerk seasoning. There are great jerk chicken recipes online; the seasoning is available at any local grocery store. Serve with *not-so-sweet* baked potato, *broken hearts* of palm or *crab* salad, and for dessert, *devil's* food cupcakes or *no-angel* food cake.

CHICKEN AND DUMPED-LINGS
For the coward who dumped me in a text.

Use your favorite recipe or buy them already prepared in the canned goods aisle at your local grocery store. Serve with a *tossed* salad. For dessert, I'd suggest lemon *dropped* cookies dunked in a little *ex*-presso. Of course, *sour grapes* or *I-call-the-shots-now* are always a must with any meal!

Beef

AGED BEEF
Old fart. Can't say I wasn't warned; he was 20 years my senior.

Prepare any aged beef (filet, porterhouse, ribeye, sirloin, or hamburger) cooked to your liking. (I'd recommend well done. This one needs to be fully cooked.) Add any side dish (mistress) and a dollar roll (cheap). There you have it: the cheap old fart with his new mistress! This recipe is dedicated to a dear friend. XO

MIS-STEAKS
Mistakes are life lessons. Learn from them and move forward.

Cook any steak to your liking—rare, medium or well done. Serve with *twice-baked* potato and a *tossed* salad. For dessert, I'd recommend the *bittersweet* chocolate cupcakes.

LET'S-ROAST-HIM POT ROAST
For the man who deserves to be slow roasted!

Any favorite pot roast recipe will do. A slow cooker (crock pot) recipe would be perfect for this meal. Serve with *whipped* potatoes and a *tossed* salad. For dessert, I'd recommend the *oh-no-you-didn't-lay-her* cake.

BABY-DON'T-COME-BACK RIBS
For those women who were all too familiar with the dry rub.

Use your favorite grilling recipe. My personal favorite is take-out from any rib or BBQ restaurant. Serve with *beet-it* salad and *shoestring* potatoes. For dessert, I'd recommend the *no-angel* food cake.

BALLS ON A PLATTER
He never had them before, so he won't miss them now!

Serve meatballs on a platter. Costco has great heat-and-serve meatballs. Add a *tossed* salad for the side dish and the *oh-no-you-didn't-lay-her* cake for dessert.

This recipe is what started the U've Been Served concept. Here's to you, my friend, and never being served again, unless it's at a five-star restaurant.

Seafood

Caught in the Act
He was never discreet. His motto: bone'm and deny!

Fried catfish served with *too-wild* rice and a *broken hearts* of palm salad. For dessert, I'd recommend the *not-so-humble* pie.

Sel-Fish
For that selfish bastard who wanted to keep me prisoner.

Fried and de-boned flounder served with *too-wild* rice and Caesar salad.

Filet of My Soul
He may have taken a knife to my heart, but here's a news flash: I healed quite nicely!

Serve with *twice-baked* potato and *crab* or *tossed* salad. For dessert, I'd recommend the *flower-less* chocolate cake.

CATCH AND RELEASE
He was the big fish I begged to get away!

SEEING-RED LOBSTER
Don't get mad get even!

CRUSTACEANS
These shellfish can also be barnacles. Once you scrape them off your boat, it's smooth sailing.

Serve any shellfish cooked to your liking with *twice-baked* potato and a *tossed* salad. This is a great opportunity to gather the girls and make reservations at Red Lobster.

RAINBOW TROUT
Two divas in one household was surely a recipe for disaster!

Serve rainbow trout, pan-seared, fried or grilled with *twice-baked* potato and *broken hearts* of palm salad. For dessert, rainbow sherbet.

Pasta

SHRIMP TRAMPÉ AND NO-ANGEL HAIR PASTA
For the ex and his mistress. They fell in love in a strip club! Not surprising.

Use any shrimp scampi and linguini recipe. Make sure the noodles are *not angel* hair! Serve with a *tossed* salad. For dessert, I'd recommend the *no-angel* food cake.

LIMP NOODLES AND NO BALLS
For the man who was never "up" for anything. In my marriage, both were useless.

Prepare your favorite spaghetti with marinara sauce recipe, minus the meat. Serve with *beet-it* salad. For dessert, I'd recommend the *not-so-stiff* lemon meringue pie.

HOT TAMALE
Yes my friend, that's what you are. So work it girlfriend!

This meal is all about the divorcee. Serve hot tamales with any salad. She calls the shots now! Always make sure you have plenty of toasts on hand. Offer *nut-less* brownies and *ex*-presso for dessert.

DINNER INSPIRATION
Today I give thanks to those who believed that I could endure anything and come back stronger.

ULTIMATE THANKSGIVING DINNER
Serve turkey with *stuff-it* stuffing, *whipped* potatoes, *not-too-sweet* potatoes, a *tossed* salad and dollar rolls, along with a bottle of your finest sour grapes. For dessert, serve *not-your-punkin'* pie.

THANKSGIVING INSPIRATION

Today, I am thankful for the friends and family that believed in my decisions and knew that I had the power to change for the better.

Boner-Petite!

Appetizers

7 LAY-HER DIP
Once was not enough. He went back six more times.

Prepare your favorite layer dip, just be sure you use seven ingredients.

DIP STICKS
For the idiot who still hasn't realized what he lost.

Carrots, celery and bell peppers, cut julienne style.

CHICKEN FINGERS
Sign language for a coward.

Kentucky Fried Chicken, McDonalds, or any grocery store frozen favorite will do nicely for this one.

SLIDERS
No matter how many years I was married, it was never easy to swallow!

Costco has heat-and-serve sliders that fit the bill.

CHILLED SHRIMP
Of course he blamed it on the cold water.

Chilled shrimp with *cock-tail* sauce

DRUNKEN SHRIMP
Always drunk and never hard!

You can find several easy-to-prepare drunken shrimp recipes online.

DRIED PRUNES WITH GOAT CHEESE
Old goat with dried up balls.

Dried prunes with a dollop of goat cheese on top.

PIG IN A BLANKET
For the man who was always under the sheets, but never under mine.

Miniature sausage wrapped in biscuit dough and baked.

DEVIL EGG
For a shell of a man. May he rot in hell!

These can be homemade or pre-made at any local grocery store.

CHICKEN LIVER
For the coward who never stood up to mama!

Chicken liver recipes are easy to find online.

CROCK-A-MOLE
For the guy that could never tell a truth!

Avocado dip.

Soups

SPLIT-UP PEA SOUP

Split it 50/50, baby! By the way, don't forget those monthly support checks!

Serve with *broken hearts* of palm salad and a dollar roll.

WHAT-A-CROCK BLACK BEAN SOUP

Are you serious, judge? I have to pay him?

Serve with a *beet-it* salad and *bread-winner*?

CRYIN' SHAME ONION SOUP

No more tears shed for this man. On to bigger and better things!

Serve with *tossed* salad and a dollar roll.

ROTTEN TOMATO SOUP

For the man who should have been thrown out with the garbage a long time ago!

Serve with grilled cheesy.

CHICKEN AND LIMP NOODLE SOUP
For the coward who could never stand up to his mother!

Serve with *tossed* salad and *crackers.*

CHICKEN AND DUMPED-LINGS
For the coward who ended it in a text. Really?

Serve with a *tossed* salad.

* Sour grapes *are recommended with all of the above menu selections*

Salads

Tossed Salad

This is for the man who thought he'd toss me aside for a younger woman. I'm happy to report, she left him, too!

Broken Hearts of Palm Salad

He may have broken my heart, but I guarantee...I'll break the bank!

Crab Salad

Finally. A crab you can share with others!

Beet-It Salad

This is for the fella who always took care of himself and never me. You know what I mean, girls!

Caesar Salad

An absolute control freak. He'll never rule the day again!

On The Side

BLACK-EYED PEAS
Traditionally known to bring good luck in the New Year.

Black eyed peas are for any woman who has been abused. It's time to see the world in a different light! We support you and we love you. Here's to a fresh start, a New Year, and new beginning!

HALF-BAKED POTATO
For the guy who was never all there!

TWICE-BAKED POTATO
Been there, done that!

NOT-SO-SWEET POTATO
Needed an anger management course!

Too-Wild Rice
For the guy you could never tame.

Whipped Potatoes
For the Mama's Boy.

Bread Winner
For years you had a soft roll. Time to try a hard one.

Stuff-It Stuffing
Goodbye forever!

Shoestring Potatoes
Always kept me on a budget.

Desserts

For that sweet taste of freedom! (DESSERTS spelled backwards is STRESSED!)

All of the desserts can be purchased at any local bakery with exception of the banana split which is easy and fun to make yourself, or DQ (Dairy Queen) it.

No-Angel Food Cake
Angel food cake. Can also be cupcakes.

Devil Food Cake
Devil's food cake. Can also be cupcakes.

Bittersweet Chocolate Cake or Cupcakes
Any dark chocolate cake will do.

Not-So-Humble Pie
Serve any pie you like—apple, cherry, etc.

LEMON DROPPED COOKIES

Lemon cookies.

FRUITCAKE

Usually sold seasonally.

NOT-SO-STIFF LEMON MERINGUE PIE

Lemon meringue pie.

OH-NO-YOU-DIDN'T LAY-HER CAKE

Any layer cake—German chocolate, raspberry, pineapple, etc.

LADY FINGERED TIRAMISU

Tiramisu

NOT-YOUR-SWEETIE PIE

Any pie that is tart. Pick fruit pies like blackberry, raspberry, boysenberry, etc.

BANANA SPLITSVILLE

Banana split

NUTLESS BROWNIES

No balls

Too-Smooth Smoothies

For the smooth talkers.

MIXED FRUIT SMOOTHIE
Never could make up his mind.

BLACKBERRY SMOOTHIE
For the man who was addicted to his phone.

BITTERSWEET SMOOTHIE
Breaking up is hard to do!

VANILLA SMOOTHIE
Always the same position—predictable and boring.

Mixed Drinks

Something to lift your spirits!

SOUR GRAPES

FAT BASTARD BEER

DIRTY BOY MARTINI

SEX ON THE BEACH

HARVEY WALL-BANG-HER

GOLD DIGGER MARGARITA

Shots

I call the shots now!

WHISKEY

VODKA

TEQUILA

SERVED WITH:

MIXED-UP NUTS

CRACKERS 'N CHEESE

GREAT-LAY'S-AHEAD POTATO CHIPS

Take Out Menu

Ex-presso Breakfast

The rich crazy bastard who could only last a minute.

Lots-of-doe-nuts and *ex*-presso.

*Dunkin' Donuts is a great source to grab-and-go. They have great espresso, too!

Couldn't-Be-Happier Happy Meal

For lunch or dinner, this is a "special meal". Go to McDonalds and pick up a Happy Meal for all of the guests. A bottle of your finest *sour grapes* would be perfect to top off this stress-free get-together.

Toasts

ALL TOASTS SHOULD BE MADE with real toast. Hold your piece of toast up to the divorcee and celebrate her independence.

Humorous

Here's to the ex-husband who said I was nuthin'
as he left the courthouse huffin' and puffin'.
Now he has nuthin', and I have it all.
Thanks for making that great judgement call!

Here's to the ex-husband, so terrible in bed.
If it wasn't for his breathing, I would have thought he was dead.

Here's to my ex. May this teach him a lesson.
The next time he cheats, he'll be poorer I'm guessin'.

Here's to my ex-husband, for now we'll call him "Bill".
He died a sudden death and forgot to change his will.
So when his kids came calling, to proclaim the big mistake,
I said, "I always loved your dad [wink]; I'll see you at the wake.

Here's to my ex-husband, the cheapest of cheap.
You've taken it all. The boobs I will keep.

Here's to my ex and his cute little honey.
She has him, and I all the money!

Here's to the 60-year-old husband who planted his seed
in a very young lady he now has to feed.
Let's toast to his patience and beginning a new life
as for me I'm in Malibu and no longer his wife.

Here's to my ex that put it in my head
I was never very sexy and terrible in bed.
So after many dates, what did I discover?
I'm damn good in bed and an excellent lover!

Here's to the hotel receipt I found in his suit
and to his personal assistant he thought was so cute,
both now unemployed and looking for hire,
while I'm running my business without an ex-liar!

Here's to the ex-husband who had to place that bet.
He spent all of our money and never paid his debt.
So when the feds came calling, I did what any good ex-wife would do.
I said, "Here's his new address and his mother's address too!"

Here's to my ex and the years I had to fake it.
Here's to my new love who showed me how to wake it!

Here's to my ex-husband and his sweet young tart,
may she forever be shackled with that grumpy old fart.

Here's to my ex-husband and his ungrateful children, too.
For years I fed and clothed them, and never saw my due.
So I'm sending all a message, I really think it's time.
Your father signed a prenup; he'll never see a dime!

Here's to my ex-husband who never had a clue.
For years I saved my money for the dream of leaving you.
Now I have enough to move forward with my life.
I am happy to report: I am finally his ex-wife!

Here's to the ex-husband who took up with the maid.
He's now picking up after her, and I am getting laid.

Here's to the ex who recently admitted
he had numerous affairs and was finally outwitted.
He was caught red-handed by a detective that I paid
and now he's paying dearly for all the women he has laid.

Here's to the ex who took on a lover.
may you never be happy in the arms of another.

Here's to my ex-husband; I was number four.
My friends gave me fair warning, but I thought that I knew more.
He wasn't very handsome, and never could get stiff.
So be careful out there ladies; he's looking for his fifth.

Here's to my ex-husband on a singles site.
He said he was a wealthy widower, looking for Mrs. Right.
Well first of all he's married, and secondly quite poor.
But you can find out for yourself; he's single now for sure.

Political

Here's to the politician who thought he'd never get caught,
and to the mistress the campaign funds bought.
May this teach him a lesson when hiding his honey.
You rarely get away with spending someone else's money.

Attorney

A toast to my attorney and her brilliant legal action.
The settlement that you brought me was pure satisfaction!

Here's to my attorney, ever so slick.
You saw what I was up against and never missed a trick.

Here's to my ex-husband, that wealthy son-of-a-bitch.
My attorney did her job and now both of us are rich!

Coming Out

Here's to the ex-husband who finally confessed.
He came out of the closet wearing my finest dress.

Here's to my ex of the same sex,
who cowardly left me with a text.
She wrote, "had enuf, done, i'm thru"
I replied, "no issue here, I'm done 2!"

Here's to my ex-husband
a mystery to me.
I never saw him coming out
and now we're history.

Inspirational

Here's to the women who never left my side
when the shit hit the fan, they held on for the ride.

Celebrate your freedom; celebrate your pride.
Celebrate the women that stood by your side.
Celebrate and show them the courage from within
for today is the day your new life will begin.

Here's to the love that never was true.
Here's to the true love searching for you.

Here's to the ex that will one day see,
the best time of his life was always with me.

Here's to my wealthy ex—forget me not—
for the memories we shared could never be bought.

Here's to the future; forget about the past.
May you soon find happiness and a love that will last.

We were children when we met and when we said I do,
and when we spoke of kids we wanted one or two,
but now the years have passed us and the dream of children too;
it's time we move on with our lives and dream with someone new.

Finish The Toast

Finish the toast is a fun way to include all the guests in the creativity of the party. Many of my friends have sent me toasts for the book. While sitting with a friend over dinner and a bottle of wine, my girlfriend suggested that those attending a *U've Been Served* party come up with their own toasts. I loved it. Here are a few *Finish the Toasts* suggestions. Fill in the blanks and bring them to the party. I encourage you to be creative, have fun, and come up with your own finish the toast!

Here's to the ex_____

_____

_____

_____

_____

_____

_____

_____

_____

_____

_____

_____

_____

_____

_____

_____

_____

_____

_____

_____

_____

_____

_____

_____

_____

Here's to_____

_____
_____
_____
_____
_____
_____
_____
_____
_____
_____
_____
_____
_____
_____
_____
_____
_____
_____
_____
_____
_____
_____
_____
_____

Create your own *U've Been Served* menu.

Breakfast

_____

_____

_____

_____

_____

_____

_____

_____

_____

_____

_____

_____

_____

_____

_____

_____

_____

_____

_____

_____

_____

_____

_____

_____

Lunch

_____
_____
_____
_____
_____
_____
_____
_____
_____
_____
_____
_____
_____
_____
_____
_____
_____
_____
_____
_____
_____

Dinner

_____
_____
_____
_____
_____
_____
_____
_____
_____
_____
_____
_____
_____
_____
_____
_____
_____
_____
_____
_____
_____
_____
_____
_____

Other

_____

_____

_____

_____

_____

_____

_____

_____

_____

_____

_____

_____

_____

_____

_____

_____

_____

_____

_____

_____

_____

_____

_____

_____

Glossary

Bacon - pig

Beet-it salad - for the do-it-yourselfer or "Get Lost!"

Bittersweet - sad it's over; left a bad taste in your mouth

Blackberry - for the man who could never put his phone down

Boner-Petite – very small penis

Bread winner - I was always the income producer!

Chicken - coward

Chicken finger - sign language for coward

Chilled shrimp - He always blamed it on the cold water.

Chopped liver pate - I was always second best!

Chopped wiener - The Lorena Bobbitt special (Disclaimer: this is *so* not legal!)

Crackers - off his rocker

Crab salad - always in a bad mood or an STD magnet

Lots of doe-nuts - rich and crazy

Dip sticks - idiot

Dog in heat - forever a cheat

Dried prunes with goat cheese - moldy old balls

Drunken shrimp - Always drunk and could never get it up!

Espresso - the one-minute man

Full of bologna - liar, liar pants on fire

French grind - not a sexual act, unless a French maid or au pair is involved

Flower-less chocolate cake - Both the flowers and the chocolates came too late.

Fruitcake - nut case

Great Lay's potato chips - fun times ahead

Half-baked - not all there

Hard-boiled - hard headed/hearted

Jerk chicken - a jerk *and* a coward

KY Jelly - tasteless

Lady fingered - my final salute in sign language

Miniature sausages - very small anatomy

Mis-steaks - any size mistake

Mixed fruit - wasn't sure what team he was playing for

Mixed nuts - he had an assortment of personalities

No-passion fruit - terrible in bed

Not-so-sweet potato - What a jerk!

Nutless brownies - no balls!

Pig in a blanket - always under the sheets, but never under *mine*

Poor boy sandwich - broke bastard

Rainbow trout - for the ex who finally came out of the closet

Roasted nuts - use your imagination

Seeing-red lobster – crustaceans; don't get mad, get even!

Rainbow sherbet - ice cream; he was very cold until he finally ex-pressed his true colors.

Shoestring potatoes - thin French fries; always lived on thin budget

Side dish - mistress

Sloppy Joe - lazy couch potato or lazy *and* messy

Sliders - very slick

Sour grapes - wine

Too-fresh berries - always a flirt

Two-wild rice - You can never tame him.

Twice-baked potato - Been there, done that!

Vanilla - plain and predicable

Whipped potatoes - Mama's boy

Wrap it up - The divorce is final!

You're toast - It's over! Serve dry or butter yourself. (Ya know what I mean, girls.)